SPAGHETTI
FOR SUZY
PETA COPLANS

Cynthia Hawarny

Houghton Mifflin Company, Boston 1993

For Cleo and Adam

Library of Congress Cataloging-in-Publication Data

Coplans, Peta.
Spaghetti for Suzy / Peta Coplans. – 1st American ed. p. cm.
Originally published: Great Britain: Andersen Press, 1992.
Summary: Although she eventually tries other foods, a young girl still likes spaghetti best.
ISBN 0-395-65232-4
[1. Spaghetti –Fiction.] I. Title.   92-21611
PZ7.C7914Sp 1993   CIP
[E] – dc20   AC

Printed in Italy

10 9 8 7 6 5 4 3 2 1

Suzy liked lots of things – dogs, cats, balloons, carnivals, and crazy bows in her hair.

At the park Suzy liked to build the highest castle in the sand-pit . . .

. . . and then squash it flat.

Most of all, Suzy liked spaghetti. She ate it every day.
"One day she'll get tired of it," her mom said.

But she didn't. Soon she wouldn't eat anything else.

Every morning Suzy's mom cooked her a mountain of spaghetti.

By bedtime it was gone.
"She'll turn into a noodle soon," her dad said. But she didn't.

In the park one day, Suzy met a cat.
"Spaghetti! Just what I need!" said the cat.

He took a long piece . . .

What do you think he did with it?

Later, Suzy met a pig.
"Spaghetti! Just what I need!" said the pig, taking two
pieces . . .

What do you think he did with them?

Along came a dog.
"Spaghetti! Just what I need!" said the dog.

He emptied the whole bowlful into his bag . . .

What do you think he did with it?

"Thanks for the spaghetti," said Suzy's friends when they came back.

"We thought you might be hungry."

Suzy looked at the fruit. The animals looked at Suzy.

"Why fruit?" asked Suzy. "I only like spaghetti."

"Apples taste of windy autumn days," said the pig.

"Cherries taste of country picnics," said the cat.

"And bananas," said the dog, "bananas taste of the wild, green jungle."

"Hmm!" said Suzy, and she ate the fruit. "ALMOST as good as spaghetti!"

"I'm still hungry," said Suzy. "We're ALL hungry!"
said the dog.

"Well, come on," said Suzy. "What are we waiting for?"

"Spaghetti for everyone!" said Suzy.

And what do you think they did with it?

Cynthia Hawarny